The Twinkling Stars

Characters

Narrator

Dad

Mom

Boy

Stars

Girl

Setting

The Carlos family's yard, one summer night

Picture Words

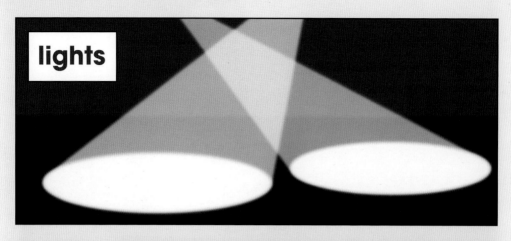

lights

night

Sight Words

are	big	like	little
look	see	up	what

shine

sky

Enrichment Words

above	bright
high	wonders

Narrator: The Carlos family is looking at the night sky. Stars shine up above the world so high.

 Dad: Look up.

 Mom: Look at the stars.

Boy: I see the stars.

 Stars: The people see us! Do they like us?

5

Girl: The stars are up so high.

 Stars: Yes! We are up high!

 Girl: The stars look so little in the sky.

 Stars: Oh, but we are not little! We are big!

Narrator: The Carlos family wonders about the bright lights twinkling in the night.

 Dad: Look up.

 Mom: Look at the stars.

 Boy: The stars are bright.

 Stars: Yes! We are bright.

Girl: What are the stars like?

 Dad: Hmmm . . .

 Mom: Hmmm . . .

 Boy: The stars are like . . . night-lights.

 Stars: We *are* night-lights.

 Girl: Stars help us see in the night.

 Stars: Yes! We shine in the night. And we twinkle, too! Twinkle, twinkle, twinkle.

Narrator: The stars twinkled above the world so high, sparkling like diamonds in the sky.

Girl: I like the stars!

 Stars: Yay! The people like us.

The End